001276317

Talent

Jackson County Library Services
Medford, OR 97501

SO-AWE-489

DATE DUE			
EC 4 '00			
APR 17 '01			
APR 27 '01			
DEC 6 '01			

11/00

**JACKSON
COUNTY**
Library Services

HEADQUARTERS
413 West Main Street
Medford, Oregon 97501

Jason's Bears

Marion Dane Bauer

Illustrated by Kevin Hawkes

Hyperion Books for Children   *New York*

JACKSON COUNTY LIBRARY SERVICES
MEDFORD, OREGON 97501

Text copyright © 2000 by Marion Dane Bauer.
Illustrations copyright © 2000 by Kevin Hawkes.

All rights reserved.

No part of this book may be reproduced or transmitted in any form
or by any means, electronic or mechanical, including photocopying,
recording, or by any information storage and retrieval
system, without written permission from the publisher.
For information address
Hyperion Books for Children,
114 Fifth Avenue,
New York, New York 10011-5690

Visit www.hyperionchildrensbooks.com, a part of the Network

Printed in Hong Kong by South China Printing Company, Ltd.

FIRST EDITION
1 3 5 7 9 10 8 6 4 2

This book is set in 18-point Cantoria.
The artwork for this book was prepared using acrylics.

Library of Congress Cataloging-in-Publication Data
Bauer, Marion Dane.
Jason's Bears/Marion Dane Bauer; illustrated by Kevin Hawkes—1st. ed.
p. cm.
Summary: Jason's enthusiasm for bears is dampened
when his big brother tells him that they are going to eat him up.
ISBN 0-7868-0356-8 (trade)—ISBN 0-7868-2303-8 (lib. bdg.)
[1. Bears—Fiction. 2. Fear—Fiction. 3. Brothers—Fiction.] I. Hawkes, Kevin, ill. II. Title.
PZ7.B3262Jas 2000
[E]—dc21   98-52968

For Little Bear

From Nonny

To Ian, who helped

—K.H.

Jason loved bears.

He loved the bears that humphed and grumphed through his favorite book, complaining about someone eating their porridge.

He loved the bears that strolled on the other side of the fence on the other side of the moat in the city zoo.

He even loved bears he'd never seen, the ones that prowled among the trees or lay curled in their dens in faraway forests.

What Jason loved most was the big of bears, the brave
of bears, the nobody-better-mess-with-me of bears, and
he thought about them day and night.

He drew pictures of bears. He sang songs about bears.
Sometimes he pretended that he was a bear. And when
he was very, very quiet, he occasionally even heard his
teddy bear growl.

One night Jason lay in bed, singing softly to himself. "Bears," he sang. "Bears, bears, bears. Big bears, little bears. Black bears, brown bears. Fuzzy bears, wuzzy bears. Bears, bears, bears."

What silliness!" Jason's big brother, Kurt, scoffed from the other side of the dark room. "You're too small and you're too scared. You shouldn't even be thinking about bears."

Jason was small and sometimes he *was* scared, but he said bravely, "I love bears."

Kurt laughed. Loudly. "*You* love bears?" he chortled. "You love *bears*," he howled. "*You* love *bears*!" he roared. "Why, the bear who lives in the bushes at the back of the yard has a mouth that's bigger than you."

"The bear who lives where?" Jason asked.
"In the bushes," his brother repeated. "If you go back there, he'll nibble your toes. One at a time. Like gumdrops."

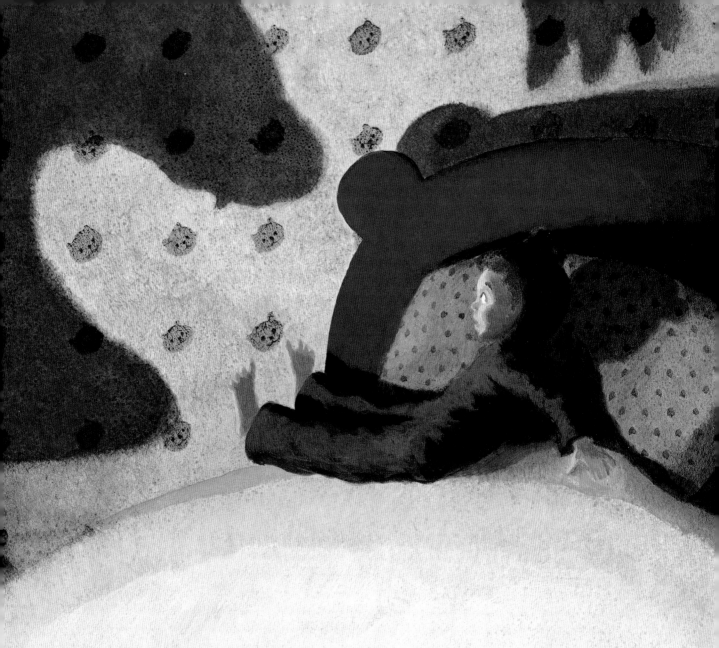

Jason curled his toes. Surely Kurt was messing with him, but still . . . he was really quite fond of his toes.

"The bear in the corner of the basement behind the furnace likes noses," Kurt went on. "They're so nice and juicy."

"That's not true!" Jason cried. Nonetheless, his hand crept up to cover his nose. Was it possible? A bear in the basement? A bear in his very own basement!

"The bear hiding between the coats in the hall closet is tall. And fat, too," Kurt added cheerfully. "He munches ears every chance he gets."

Jason didn't say another word. He just curled his toes, covered his nose, and put his remaining hand over one ear. The other ear just sat there on the side of his head, trembling.

"And right now," Kurt whispered, "the biggest bear of all is waiting under your bed. Some day he's going to swallow you whole."

"Are you sure it's not *your* bed he's under?" Jason asked, his voice rather small.

But Kurt only laughed. "Bears never eat big guys like me," he said. "We're too tough."

Jason said, "Oh," and for the rest of the night he lay very still, keeping his toes and nose and ears, in fact, keeping his entire self, covered.

Maybe, he thought, you do have to be big to love bears.

After that, Jason quit drawing pictures of bears. He quit singing songs about bears. Especially, he quit pretending he *was* a bear. And when his teddy bear disappeared, he didn't bother looking for him. Mostly, he just sat around, trying not to think about bears.

One day, when Jason was sitting on the back steps thinking very hard about nothing at all, Kurt came around the corner of the house wearing a big smile. "We baked gingerbread cookies in school today," he announced, "and I made one especially for you."

"For me?" Jason asked.

"For you?" Kurt repeated. "I hope it doesn't eat you." And he handed Jason a golden-brown cookie and ran inside, snickering.

The cookie was shaped like a bear.

The bear's claws were candies, red as blood. His ears were juicy raisins, big enough to hear Jason's heart beating. The nose was a lump of licorice ready to snuffle up the scent of the boy. The bear's currant eyes stared right at Jason, and its white-frosting teeth glistened.

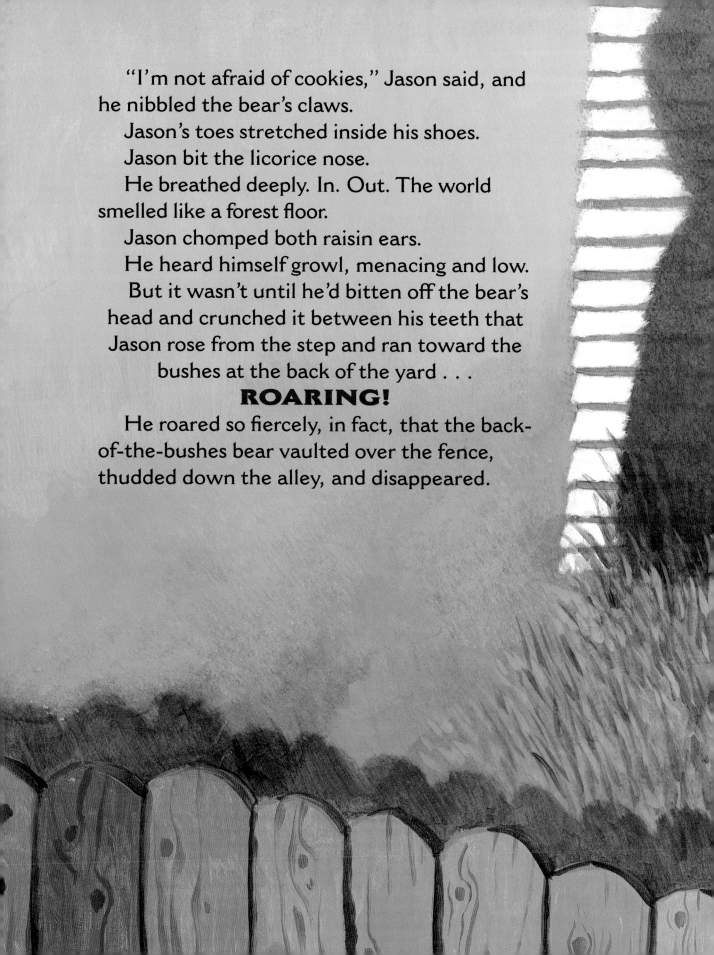

"I'm not afraid of cookies," Jason said, and he nibbled the bear's claws.

Jason's toes stretched inside his shoes.

Jason bit the licorice nose.

He breathed deeply. In. Out. The world smelled like a forest floor.

Jason chomped both raisin ears.

He heard himself growl, menacing and low.

But it wasn't until he'd bitten off the bear's head and crunched it between his teeth that Jason rose from the step and ran toward the bushes at the back of the yard . . .

ROARING!

He roared so fiercely, in fact, that the back-of-the-bushes bear vaulted over the fence, thudded down the alley, and disappeared.

"That's better!" Jason said, and he took another bite of the cookie.

Which was when he remembered the bear in the dark corner behind the furnace.

When Jason marched down the stairs calling, "Here, bear. Come out, bear," the basement bear was so surprised that he climbed into the furnace and disappeared in a puff of smoke.

"Good riddance!" Jason told the bear. And before heading for the closet, he took another bite of the cookie.

The closet bear didn't even wait to be seen. He scattered winter coats the length of the hall and mittens and scarves across the front yard.
"What kind of game are you playing now?" Kurt sneered.

But Jason didn't answer. He just popped the last of the cookie into his mouth and strode toward his room, chewing.

When he got to the door, he stopped and stood there, very quiet.

The under-bed bear was quiet, too. Jason licked the cookie crumbs from his lips.

"I'm the big of boys," he whispered. And he stepped into the room.

"I'm the brave of boys," he declared, a little more loudly. And he walked right up to the bed.

"I'm the nobody-better-mess-with-me of boys," he bellowed. And he got down onto his hands and knees and peered beneath the bed.

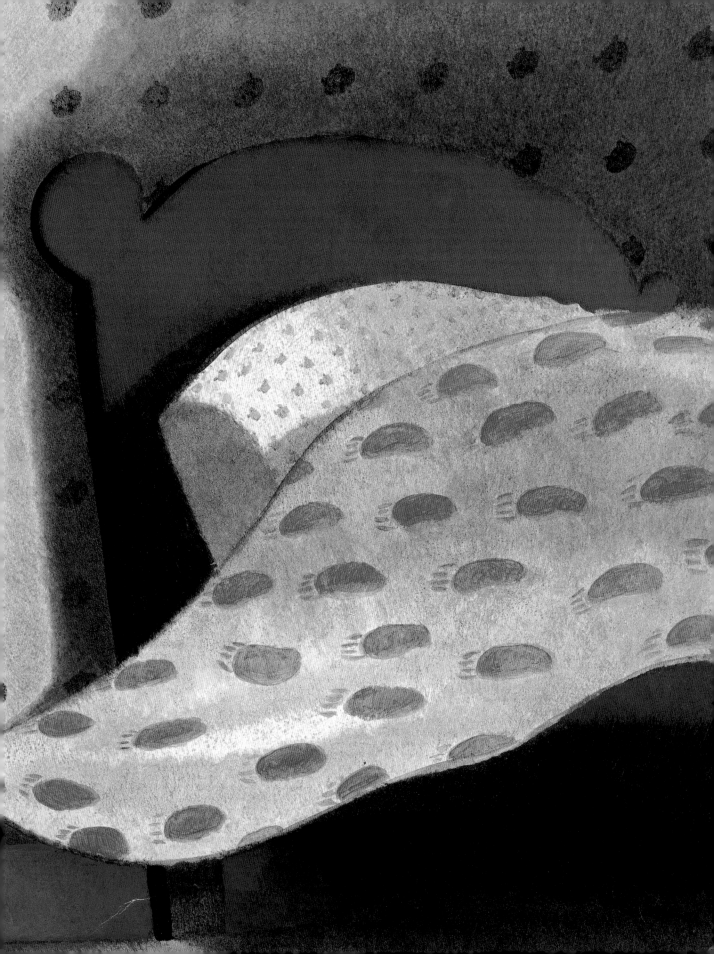

The under-bed place looked like a cave. It smelled like dust and fur. It was as dark as the inside of a very big belly. And the bear who lay curled in the farthest corner, hugging Jason's teddy, said rather timidly, "You know, I really do love boys."

"And I love bears," Jason replied, gently prying his teddy from between the bear's paws. "But I don't believe I care to have one living beneath my bed."

"Where do you want me to go?" the bear asked.

"Well," Jason said. "You know," he said. "I do have a big brother . . ."

That night Jason lay in his bed, his teddy bear tucked
under one arm, when a growl came out of the darkness.
"Did you hear that?" Kurt asked.

"I heard," Jason said. "I think the bear is under *your* bed now."

"Naw," Kurt replied. "It couldn't be," he said, though his voice quavered just a bit. "I never heard of a bear living beneath a bed."

"Didn't you?" Jason asked sweetly. "Well, then maybe there isn't one, after all."

And smiling to himself, Jason rolled
over, gave his teddy a squeeze, and slipped
into a peaceful sleep . . .
    where he dreamed of bears in books,
    of bears in zoos,
    and of bears prowling among the trees or
lying curled in their dens in faraway forests.

❧ JASON'S GINGER BEAR COOKIES ❧

½ cup hot water

1 teaspoon baking soda

1 teaspoon salt

1 teaspoon ginger

1½ teaspoon cinnamon

½ teaspoon ground cloves

½ teaspoon nutmeg

1 cup sugar

1 cup shortening

1 cup dark molasses

2 eggs

5½ cups flour

Stir the baking soda, the salt, and all the spices into the hot water. Set your spice mixture aside and mix the sugar and shortening together until they are smooth. Then, stir the spice mixture, the molasses, the eggs, and the flour into your sugar and shortening mixture. If necessary, you may add up to a half cup more flour to make a stiff dough for rolling. Cover the dough and chill it in the refrigerator for at least an hour. Once the dough is chilled, roll it on a floured surface and cut out bears.

You can use red-hots for claws, licorice bits for noses, raisins for ears, currants for eyes. Perhaps you will think of other decorating ideas. Sprinkle the cookies lightly with sugar and bake on a greased pan (or a nonstick one) at 350°F for 10 to 12 minutes. Put the hot cookies on a rack and, once they are cool, nibble the toes, chew the ears, and bite the noses. Then gobble your bears down and discover how fierce you feel.